LAKESHORE SC
P9-CAJ-576
E
A
Astley, Judy
When one cat woke up
Z8217
DATE DUE
MAR 06 1998
MAY 05 1998
PERMA-BOUND
© THE BAKER & TAYLOR CO.

When One Cat Woke Up

For Zelda, Layla,
and Jon

First published in the United States 1990
by Dial Books for Young Readers
A Division of Penguin Books USA Inc.
375 Hudson Street
New York, New York 10014
Published in Great Britain by Frances Lincoln

Printed in Hong Kong
First Edition
E
1 3 5 7 9 10 8 6 4 2

Library of Congress Cataloging in Publication Data
Astley, Judy. When one cat woke up.
Summary: A cat wakes up and romps through the house,
wrecking things in numerical order.
[1. Cats—Fiction. 2. Counting] I. Title.
PZ7.A848Wh 1990 [E] 89-23260
ISBN 0-8037-0782-7

When One Cat Woke Up

A Cat Counting Book

Judy Astley

Dial Books for Young Readers / New York

When one cat
woke up

1

she stole . . .

two fish

2

and fought with . . .

three teddy bears

3

and crumpled . . .

four shirts

4

and broke . . .

five cups

5

and unraveled . . .

six balls of wool

6

and tangled . . .

H
h
b
B
F
f
A
a

seven sheep

and knocked over . . .

eight flowers

8

and frightened . . .

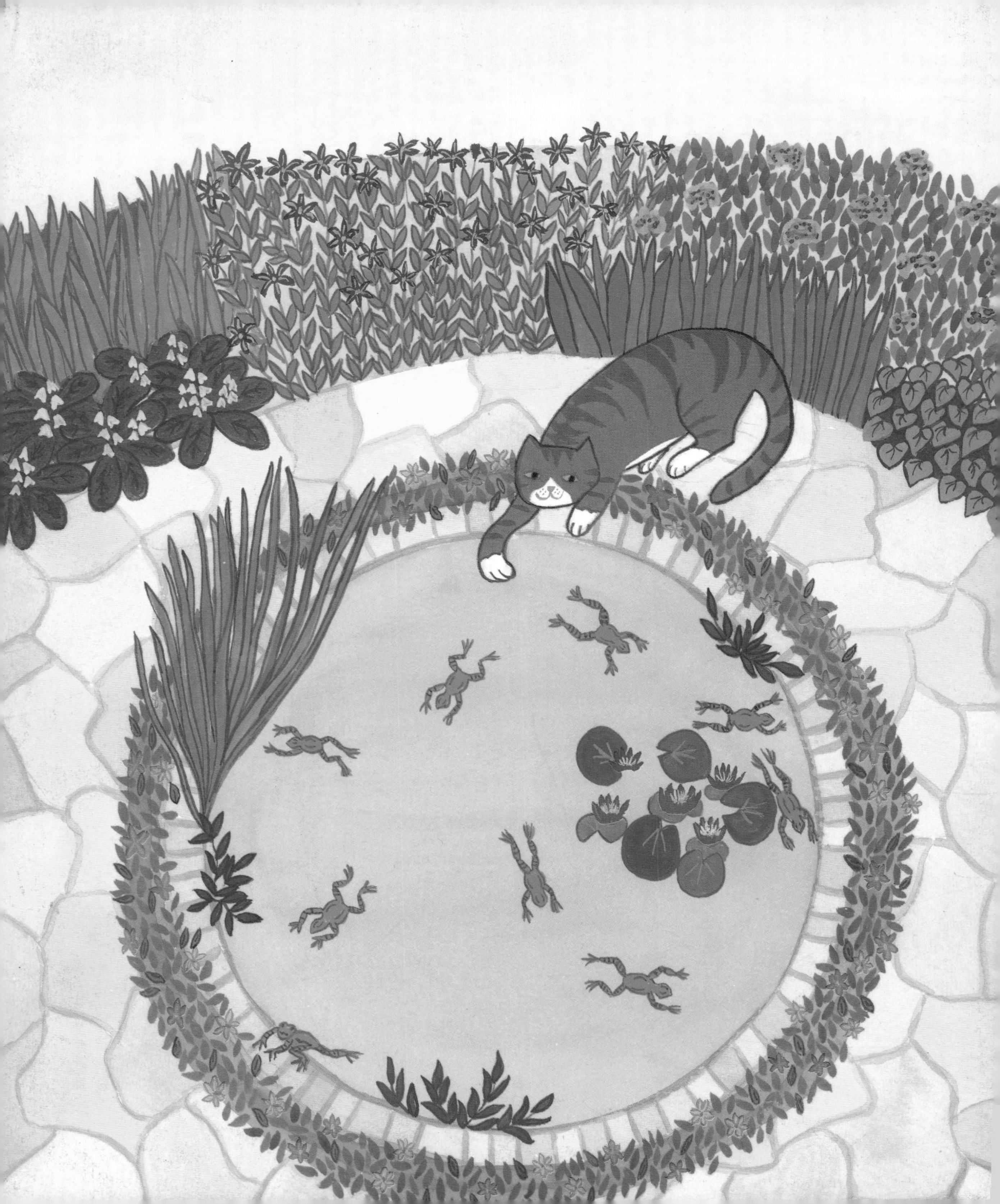

nine frogs

9

and left . . .

10

ten muddy pawprints

on her way back to sleep.

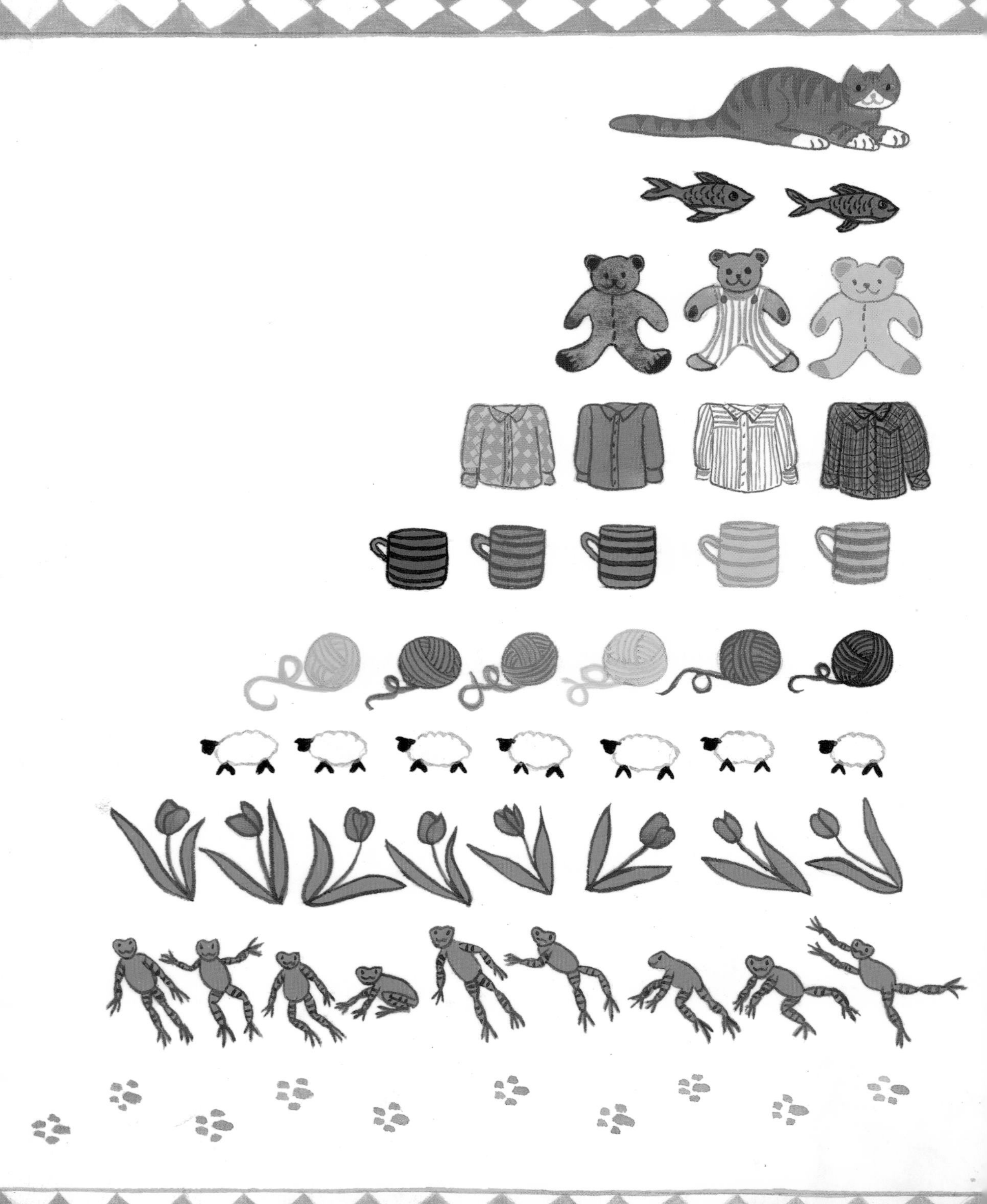

1 cat

2 fish

3 teddy bears

4 shirts

5 cups

6 balls of wool

7 sheep

8 flowers

9 frogs

10 muddy pawprints